Ollie Bear's

Adventures with the Rainbow Heart Light

The Little Green Frog

Written by Tracey O'Mara

Illustrated by Sherae Kim

Balboa Press books may be ordered through booksellers or by contacting:

Balboa Press
A Division of Hay House
1663 Liberty Drive
Bloomington, IN 47403
www.balboapress.com
1 (877) 407-4847

Because of the dynamic nature of the Internet, any web addresses or links contained in this book may have changed since publication and may no longer be valid. The views expressed in this work are solely those of the author and do not necessarily reflect the views of the publisher, and the publisher hereby disclaims any responsibility for them.

Any people depicted in stock imagery provided by Thinkstock are models, and such images are being used for illustrative purposes only. Certain stock imagery © Thinkstock.

ISBN: 978-1-5043-5658-9 (sc)
ISBN: 978-1-5043-5659-6 (e)

Library of Congress Control Number: 2016906576

Print information available on the last page.

Balboa Press rev. date: 06/16/2016

BALBOA.
PRESS
A DIVISION OF HAY HOUSE

Once upon a time in a quaint little town called Joyville, Ollie Bear and his friends Lewey Bear and Oshi Bear were playing outdoors.

It was a beautiful sunny day. It was such a warm day that Ollie Bear and his friends decided to go down to the pond at the bottom of Grandma Bear's garden with their buckets and fishing nets to catch frogs.

Ollie Bear loved frogs. In the pond, he saw a tiny little frog swimming by. The little frog popped his head up and Ollie Bear dipped his fishing net into the pond and caught the little frog in it.

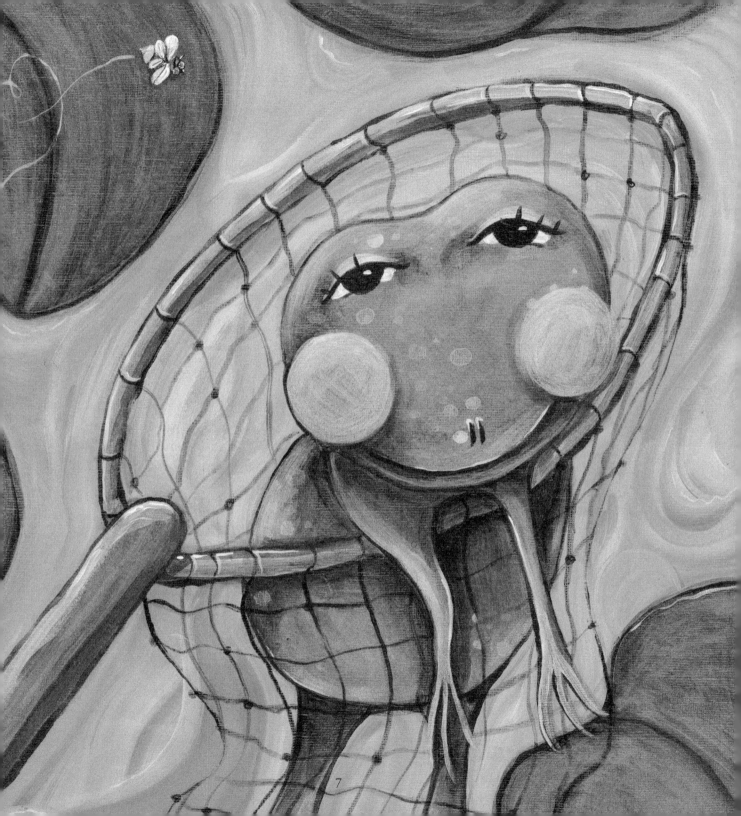

He put the frog in his bucket with a tiny bit of water and a rock for the little frog to sit on.

Then Ollie Bear and his friends ran back up the garden to play on the swings. As they ran past Grandpa Bear and Grandma Bear watching them from the porch, Grandma Bear said, "Ollie Bear, don't forget to give your little frog more water, it is a very hot day."

"I won't, Grandma Bear," Ollie Bear said.

Ollie Bear and his friends lost track of time as they happily played on the swings, the slide, and in the sandpit.

Then suddenly Ollie Bear said, "Oh no! I forgot to give my little frog more water!" He ran to the little frog who looked very sick. The water had all dried up.

"What should we do, Ollie Bear?" Lewey Bear said.

"Let's ask Grandma Bear, she'll know what to do,"

And she did. Grandma Bear gave the little
frog more water straight away.

She then said to Ollie Bear and his friends, "let's close our eyes, gather up all of our love from within our hearts, and imagine a healing green light. The Rainbow Heart Light Angels, Clair Bear and Sarah Bear will help us send that light to the little frog so that he can feel better."

As the little bears stood there with their eyes shut, Ollie Bear peeked out of one eye and was delighted to see that the little frog was getting better. He was so excited he shouted out with glee, "Look, Grandma Bear, it is working!"

Now that the little frog was feeling much better, Grandma
Bear thought that it was best to take the little frog back
to his home. As they released the frog, Ollie Bear asked
Grandma Bear if the Rainbow Heart Light Angels
would have anything to say about the little frog.

Grandma Bear said, "yes, Ollie Bear. When you took the little frog from the pond, you became responsible for his life. You have to care for him and give him everything he needs. The Rainbow Heart Light teaches us that all life is important, no matter how tiny that life may be."

Grandma Bear's Guide

How to Use the Colors of the Rainbow Heart Light

Grandma Bear likes to use certain colors for different things, but you can use any color that you like.

Step 1: "First, pick a color"

Step 2: "close your eyes"

Step 3: "imagine that color is filled with all of the love in your heart"

Step 4: "think of the person, this can be even yourself, animal, or situation you would like to help"

Step 5: "picture that person, animal, or situation surrounded by that color"

Grandma Bear's Color Chart:

Green is very soothing and healing. You can use Green for someone that is injured and all the animals and plants on the earth.

Pink for any little bear (person) that isn't feeling very well, is worried, or going through a difficult time in their life.

Purple to inspire ourselves and others to use our creative gifts.

Blue to help ourselves and others feel calm in uncomfortable situations and to help all of the creatures in the ocean.

Yellow to spread happiness. It helps us to feel happy and goofy. You can also send yellow to help all of the little bumble bees, after all, they have a very important job to do!

Orange is for joy and laughter. It also gives us all energy and helps to empower and uplift our spirits.

Red is to help us and others feel strong in any situation and helps us feel protected in challenging times.

Gold and White to send to all of our loved ones that are no longer here on earth with us.

Turquoise is a special color we can send to ourselves. Using turquoise, we can wrap ourselves up with love and it reminds us that we are all perfect just the way we are.

CₘSₗA information can be obtained
at www.ICGtesting.com
Printed in the USA
LVOW05s0408080716
495539LV00008B/10/P

9 781504 356589